THE LION AND THE JACKAL

Children and adults alike, we all love stories. When we share a story with children we can help them to explore important areas of human experience and encourage them in their spiritual and moral development. The Greek myths, stories from the Bible, and the countless tales of the world's many religions show that humanity has long used story to communicate its deepest values and codes of behaviour. The magical qualities of a story speak directly to our hearts and illustrate and share profound truths. Imaginatively entering another's world, we return with insights to apply to our own lives.

We have enjoyed writing and illustrating this story from the Buddhist tradition. We hope you and your children will enjoy it too.

Adiccabandhu & Padmasri

Published in association with
The Clear Vision Trust
by Windhorse Publications
11 Park Road
Birmingham B13 8AB

Text and illustrations
© Clear Vision Trust 1998
Design Dhammarati
Illustrations Adiccabandhu
Printed by Interprint Ltd,
Marsa, Malta

British Library Cataloguing in
Publication Data. A catalogue
record for this book is available
from the British Library
ISBN 1 899579 13 3

THE LION
AND THE JACKAL

WINDHORSE PUBLICATIONS

One day a young lion was hunting in the hills when he found a cave. "What a good home this would make for our family." he thought.

Down below he could see the river.
Wild deer were drinking there.
"Each morning we could run down and catch some breakfast," he thought.
"In fact I'll go right now!"

As the lion raced down the hillside towards the river
all the other animals ran for safety.

The lion wanted to catch a deer.

He hurled himself into the air over a bush – and missed.

Instead, he landed right in the middle of some deep mud!
"Oh no!" he cried.

He tried to pull his legs out of the mud but the more he
struggled, the deeper he sank.
The mud now came up to his stomach.

"Help! I'm stuck!" he cried.
"Perhaps, if I roar loud enough, someone might hear me."
And he roared and roared with all his might.
But no one came.

For a whole week, he lay trapped in the mud.
"I'm going to die here," he thought.

Suddenly, a jackal's grey head peeped out from under the bush.
"Please, help me," gasped the lion.
"Why should I?" replied the jackal, "you only want to eat me."

"If you help me now I will always be your friend," said the lion.

"How do I know I can trust you?" asked the jackal.

The jackal looked at the lion. If she did not help him he would slowly die. "Do you promise?" she asked.

"Yes, I promise," said lion.

"All right," she said, "I trust you."

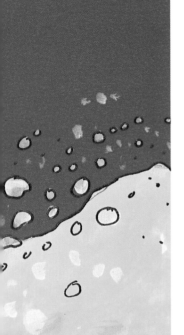

Cautiously the jackal crept across the mud
towards the lion. Then she began to dig.
All morning she dug.
"I can just see your knees now, lion," she said,
"but your paws are still stuck. It will take me all
day to dig you out."

"Hmmm! It would help if we had some water,"
she thought.
At the edge of the river she found a coconut
shell. She carried water and poured it around
the lion's legs until the mud began to soften.

"You try to loosen the mud around your paws," she said, "and I'll push from under your stomach.
One last effort and you'll be free."

The jackal pushed and the lion pulled.

At last his great paws began to move.
With a mighty heave, the lion pulled himself out of the mud.

The jackal stood back.
Had she had been right to trust him?
"Thank you for helping me," said the lion.
"Thank you for trusting me.
From now on, I will always be your friend.
You have my word as king of the beasts."

From that day on the lion and the jackal were friends. They hunted together and shared all the food they caught.

One day as the lion and the jackal lay on the ledge talking, the lion said, "Why don't both our families live here together? We could shelter in the caves and eat our food out here on the ledge. We could even take turns to look after the little ones."

"What a great idea!" replied the jackal.
"I'm sure our families would be happy living here together."

The next day the lion family
and the jackal family all moved
into their new home.

Soon the lion cubs and the
jackal pups were making
friends, laughing and playing
together in the sun.

When the summer came the river began to run dry.
The lush green grass became shrivelled and yellow and the wild
deer moved away.
Food became scarce and the lion and the jackal had caught
nothing for days. Everyone felt cross and hungry.

One day, two of the older lions sat on the ledge.
"Look at our young lion wasting his time hunting with that
jackal. No wonder we're hungry," one of them grumbled.
"Yes," added the other. "It's because of the jackals that there is
not enough food to go round. It's time we got rid of them."

But one of the jackals heard the old lions complaining

He went off at once to tell his friends.

"The lions are saying that it's our fault there is no food," he said.

"I don't know what they're talking about?" one of them grumbled.

"Those smelly old lions do nothing but sleep all day. Their young lion would catch nothing without our jackal to help."

Before long other tales were being told. The lion cubs and jackal pups began to fight when they played together.

"Don't play with those noisy jackal pups!" mother lions told their cubs.

"You're not to bring those rough lion cubs back to our den!" said the mother jackals.

When anything went wrong the lions would blame the jackals, and the jackals would blame the lions.

As the hot season went on food became more and more scarce.
One day one of the old lions spotted a jackal pup with a bone.
"Those jackals must be catching food and not telling us," he growled.
He pushed the puppy out of the way and snatched the bone.

He took the bone to show the young lion.

"Look at this!" he complained.

"Those sly jackals are catching meat and keeping it for themselves.

The young lion looked at the bone. He had caught nothing for days. Where had the jackal puppy got the bone from?

"The mother jackal is my friend and I trust her," he said, "but this is a puzzle. I will ask her about it."

He took the bone over to where the mother jackal sat. A little pup was crying.

"And then that old lion came and took my bone away," he whimpered. The jackal shook her head at the lion.

"This is no good," she said. "How can we trust the lions when they pick on our little pups? If we cannot live happily together we shall have to leave!"

"Where did the pup get this food from?" asked the lion. "Didn't we agree to share all our food?"

"This bone isn't fresh food," explained the mother jackal. "Like all good jackals, the pup buried it weeks ago. She wanted to save it for another day."

"Of course; now I understand," said the lion. "I knew that we could trust each other. All this telling tales has caused a lot of harm and unhappiness."

That night, the lion called his family together.
"Do you remember when I went missing for a
week?" he asked.
"Yes," they replied. "When you came back
you started sharing our food with that jackal."
"I will tell you what happened to me that
week," said the lion.
And he told the lions how the jackal had dug
him out of the mud and saved his life.

"I wouldn't be here now if it wasn't for her," he said.
The lions hung their heads in shame.
"We had no idea," they said. "Thank goodness the jackal trusted
you. We must go and thank her."

From that day on, the two families lived happily together. Often
they would tell the story of how the jackal had saved the lion.
And they never forgot how to be good friends to each other.

notes

About the story

The story of the Lion and the Jackal is one of more than 500 Jataka tales recorded in early Buddhist scriptures. It illustrates the importance of generosity and trust within friendship.

The Jataka tales are said to have been related by the Buddha to his disciples. The word Jataka (pronounced jah-ta-ka) means "relating to the birth"; these stories are traditionally said to be accounts of the past lives of the Buddha as he followed the path towards Enlightenment. Buddhists today do not necessarily see these accounts as historically true, but as pointing to deeper truths about what it means to be a human being. Most of them were probably adopted from Indian folklore because they illustrated Buddhist principles. All of them demonstrate the central Buddhist teaching of the Law of Karma: that actions have consequences. Just as selfish actions lead to suffering, selfless actions lead to true happiness.

Telling this story, the Buddha explained to some of his young disciples that it came from one of his previous lives, when he was the lion and his friend Ananda was the jackal. In the original story, the jackal is male. The young pupils would have known that the Buddha and Ananda had been close friends and companions for many years.

Exploring the story

Adults can enhance the natural process of learning by encouraging children to talk about the story. Open-ended questions will encourage children to make an imaginative entry into the world of the story to empathize with the characters, and to make connections with their own lives.

Which part of the story did you like best, and why?

Which of the people in the story would you most/least like to be? Why?

What do you think would have happened if ...
- the lion had broken his promise to the jackal?
- the lion hadn't asked the jackal about the bone?
- someone had really cheated with the food?

Themes to develop

Friendship and Trust
Talk about
- a time when you have trusted a friend. What happened?
- a time when someone has trusted you
- people you trust and why

Helping others
Talk about
- when you need help and who helps you
- how you thank the people who help you
- in what ways you help other people

Gossip and telling lies
Talk about
- how you feel when people say things about you that aren't true
- a time when passing on stories, or telling tales, has caused unhappiness

Being sorry
Talk about
- what it means to apologise
- a time when you were sorry for something you had said or done – how you showed you were sorry

BUDDHISM is one of the fastest-growing spiritual traditions in the Western world. Throughout its 2,500-year history, it has always succeeded in adapting its mode of expression to suit whatever culture it has encountered.

WINDHORSE PUBLICATIONS aims to continue this tradition as Buddhism comes to the West. It publishes works by authors who not only understand the Buddhist tradition but are also familiar with Western culture and the Western mind. Parents and teachers will find a wealth of background information amongst these books.

Introductory Books

Suitable introductory books include
Introducing Buddhism
by Chris Pauling

Who is the Buddha?
by Sangharakshita

What is the Dharma?
The Essential Teachings of the Buddha
by Sangharakshita

Change Your Mind
A Practical Guide to Buddhist Meditation
by Paramananda

These and many other titles are available from Windhorse Publications

Orders & catalogues

Windhorse Publications
11 Park Road,
Birmingham,
B13 8AB, UK
Tel [+44] (0)121 449 9191

Windhorse Publications Inc
540 South 2nd West,
Missoula, MT 59802, USA
Tel [+1] 406 327 0034

Windhorse Books
PO Box 574, Newtown,
NSW 2042, Australia
Tel [+61] (0)2 9519 8826

Clear Vision

The Clear Vision Trust is a Buddhist educational charity which promotes understanding of Buddhism through the visual media. Clear Vision's education team produces a range of resources, books, and videos to support high quality religious education and spiritual, moral, social, and cultural development. It also provides in-service training on Buddhism for classroom teachers.

Recommended videos include the award-winning
Buddhism for Key Stage Two
and
The Monkey King and Other Tales

Clear Vision
16–20 Turner Street,
Manchester M1 4DZ, UK
Tel [+44] (0)161 839 9579

The FWBO

Windhorse Publications and Clear Vision are associated with the Friends of the Western Buddhist Order (FWBO). Through its sixty centres on five continents, members of the Western Buddhist Order offer meditation classes and other activities for the general public and for more experienced students. Centres also welcome school parties and teachers interested in Buddhism.

If you would like more information about the FWBO please contact
London Buddhist Centre
51 Roman Road,
London, E2 0HU, UK
Tel [+44] (0)181 981 1225

Aryaloka Retreat Center
Heartwood Circle,
Newmarket, NH 03857,
USA

In the same series

Siddhartha and the Swan

Quarrelling over a wounded swan, the young Prince Siddhartha helps his cousin learn about kindness to animals. Beautifully illustrated, this magical tale from the Buddhist tradition will entrance the younger reader.
Illustrated by Adiccabandhu

ISBN 1 899579 10 9
£5.99/$10.95

The Monkey King

A stirring jungle tale of greed, heroism, and mangoes. Beautifully illustrated, this delightful tale from the Buddhist tradition is retold in a style that will enchant the young reader.
Illustrated by Adiccabandhu

ISBN 1 899579 09 5
£5.99/$10.95

About the authors

Adiccabandhu is an ordained Buddhist. An author and illustrator, he works for the Clear Vision Trust, a Buddhist educational charity. He has over twenty years experience in education as teacher, trainer, and producer of educational resources, and has four grown-up children of his own.

Padmasri is an ordained Buddhist who has enjoyed a long career in primary education, both as teacher and trainer. A mother with grown-up children of her own, she now works for the Clear Vision Trust.